Jon Scieszka's TRUCKTOWN
KAT'S MYSTERY GIFT

WRITTEN BY JON SCIESZKA

CHARACTERS AND ENVIRONMENTS DEVELOPED BY THE

DAVID SHANNON   **LOREN LONG**   **DAVID GORDON**

ILLUSTRATION CREW:

Executive producer: Keytoon, Inc. in association with Animagic S.L.

Creative supervisor: Sergio Pablos ○ Drawings by: Juan Pablo Navas ○ Color by: Isabel Nadal

Color assistant: Gabriela Lazbal ○ Art director: Karin Paprocki

READY-TO-ROLL

ALADDIN

NEW YORK   LONDON   TORONTO   SYDNEY

CH

ALADDIN

An imprint of Simon & Schuster

Children's Publishing Division

1230 Avenue of the Americas, New York, NY 10020

First Aladdin paperback edition October 2009

For information about special discounts for bulk purchases, please contact Simon & Schuster Special Sales at 1-866-506-1949
or business@simonandschuster.com.

The Simon & Schuster Speakers Bureau can bring authors to your live event. For more information or to book an event
contact the Simon & Schuster Speakers Bureau at 1-866-248-3049 or visit our website at www.simonspeakers.com.

The text of this book was set in Truck King. / Manufactured in the United States of America / 10 9 8 7 6 5 4 3 2 1

Library of Congress Cataloging-in-Publication Data / Scieszka, Jon.

Kat's mystery gift / written by Jon Scieszka ; characters and environments developed by Design Garage: David Shannon,
Loren Long, David Gordon. – 1st Aladdin Paperbacks ed. / p. cm. – (Trucktown) (Ready-to-roll)

Summary: The trucks speculate about what could be inside a beautifully wrapped gift box.

[1. Gifts—Fiction. 2. Trucks—Fiction.] I. Design Garage. II. Title.

PZ7.S41267Kat 2009 / [E]—dc22 / 2007027801

ISBN 978-1-4169-4143-9 (pbk) / ISBN 978-1-4169-4154-5 (lib)

Kat has a gift.

The gift is red.

And square.
And a mystery.

"What is inside?"
asks Gabby.

"That," says Kat, "is the mystery."

"I guess it is a new horn,"
says Gabby.
"Could be," says Kat.

"I guess it is
a new ball,"
says Rosie.

"Could be," says Kat.

"I guess it is new tires," says Pete.

"Could be,"
says Kat.

"New sirens?" guesses Pat.
"New lights?" guesses Lucy.

"Could be ... and could be," says Kat.

"But it could be a jewel,"
says Kat.

"Or a cloud..."

"WOW!"

says Gabby.

"Open it, open it,
open it now!"
they all cheer.
"We could . . . ," says Kat.